Jason
and the
Golden Fleece

A Greek Legend

Retold by Alan Trussell-Cullen

Illustrated by Francis Phillipps

DOMINIE PRESS
Pearson Learning Group

Many years ago, in the kingdom of Thebes, there were two princes, Aeson and his younger brother Pelias. When their father died, Aeson was made king of Thebes. But Pelias was jealous of his brother. So he had Aeson locked away in prison and made himself the king.

Aeson had a young son named
Jason. Jason's mother was afraid
that Pelias would have her son killed.
So she made one of her servants
swear that she would take Jason
out of the country.
Safely away from his
Uncle Pelias, Jason grew
up to be a wise and strong
young man.

One day Jason came back to Thebes and demanded that Pelias return the crown to his father.

Pelias laughed at him. "I could have you killed," he said. "But instead, I will challenge you to a dare. Travelers tell stories of a Golden Fleece. If you can find it and bring it to me, I will give the crown to your father."

"I accept your dare!" said Jason.

Pelias knew that the Golden Fleece belonged to King Aeetes, a fierce warrior, and everyone who had tried to take it from him had been killed.

First, Jason built a magnificent ship for his journey. He called the ship *Argo*, which means *swift*. He gathered together some of the strongest and bravest men in the land to sail his ship. He called them his Argonauts.

Now they were ready to set sail, but Jason still did not know where to start looking for the Golden Fleece. He placed his hand on the ship's figurehead, which had been carved from a magic oak tree. The figurehead began to speak. "Go ask King Phineus, for he knows where the Golden Fleece is," the voice said.

Jason shouted. "We sail for the castle of King Phineus!"

The *Argo* sailed for many days until it reached the castle.

King Phineus welcomed Jason warmly. But Jason was puzzled. There was plenty of food in the castle, yet everyone seemed to be starving.

"You shall see why," said King Phineus.

A magnificent feast was spread on the banquet table. But before anyone could start to eat, a flock of hideous birds flew into the castle. They fought and pecked and scratched at everyone with their beaks and their claws.

"It's the Harpies!" shouted King Phineus. "Quick! Hide under the table or they will eat us as well as the food!"

Jason leaped to his feet and drew his sword. "Argonauts, prepare to attack!" he shouted.

Jason and his men lashed out with their swords, and feathers flew in all directions. Soon the Harpies had had enough. They flew off, shrieking as they went.

"At last we can eat!" said King Phineus. "How can I thank you?"

"Please tell us how to find the Golden Fleece," Jason said.

King Phineus turned pale. "Very well. It hangs in the Land of Colchis," he said. "But there is dangerous magic in that place. First you must pass the Clashing Cliffs. They are terrifying enough to make a brave man tremble with fear like a little child."

Jason stood up. "We do not know what fear is! Come!" He called to the Argonauts. "We head for the Clashing Cliffs immediately!"

The Clashing Cliffs were a terrifying sight.
Two cliffs rose up on either side with only
a narrow stretch of water between them.
Huge waves crashed against the cliff walls.
Hot molten rock flowed down the cliff face,
and red-hot boulders plunged into the sea all
around them.

"If the waves don't smash our ship, the boulders will!" cried one of the Argonauts.

"Wait!" said Jason. "See those seagulls? They have found a way through. We must follow them. Pull on your oars as you have never rowed before!"

The Argonauts pulled on their oars, and their ship darted this way and that as they followed the seagulls through the narrow gap between the Clashing Cliffs.

On the other side, the sea was calm. Soon they came to the island of Colchis, where they were met by King Aeetes.

"I have come to claim the Golden Fleece!" declared Jason.

King Aeetes just laughed. "Then first you must fight my soldiers," he said.

King Aeetes put his hand into his pocket and pulled out a handful of dragon's teeth. Then he threw them into the air. They were magic teeth, and as soon as they touched the ground, they turned into an army of fierce warriors. Jason's twelve Argonauts were outnumbered a hundred to one.

Nevertheless, Jason drew his sword. "We fought the Harpies! We battled the Clashing Cliffs! And we can deal with a handful of teeth!"

His men drew their swords, too. They battled and fought fiercely, and soon Jason and his Argonauts had beaten the fierce warriors.

Jason looked around. On the top of a nearby hill was a single tree, and hanging from the tree was a fleece made of gleaming gold. It was the Golden Fleece! But guarding the tree was a ferocious dragon!

Jason turned to his men. "I have to fight the dragon on my own in order to claim the Golden Fleece. Wait for me by the *Argo* until I return with the prize."

Jason made his way up the hill. On the way he met a beautiful young woman. She was the king's daughter, and her name was Princess Medea.

"I watched you battle the dragon-tooth warriors," she said. "You are indeed a brave man. Marry me, and I will help you retrieve the Golden Fleece with my magic."

Jason shook his head. "I must retrieve the Golden Fleece by my own strength. Wait for me. If I am successful, I will marry you."

The dragon had been watching Jason the whole time. It sat crouched on the edge of a cliff near the Golden Fleece, waiting to pounce on Jason if he came too close.

Jason had been watching the dragon the whole time, too, wondering how the dragon could be defeated.

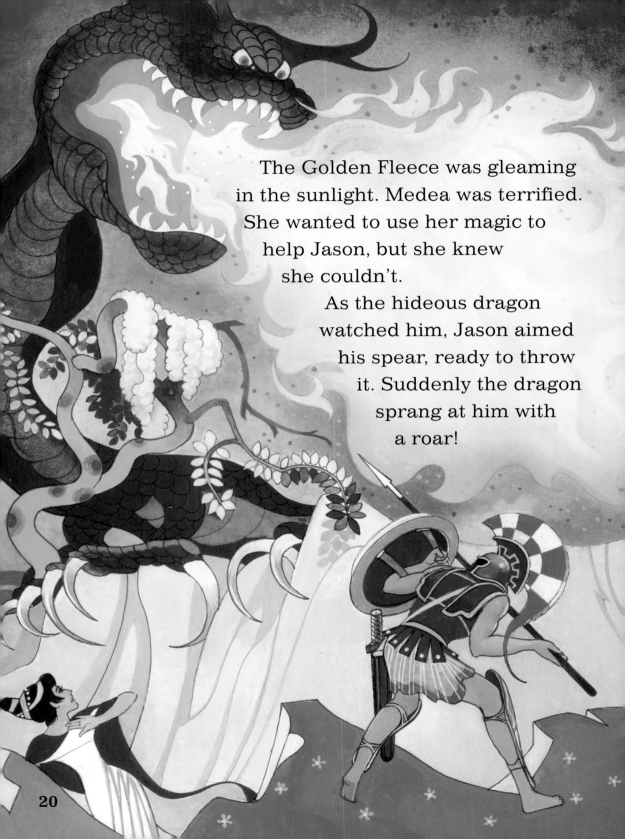

The Golden Fleece was gleaming
in the sunlight. Medea was terrified.
She wanted to use her magic to
help Jason, but she knew
she couldn't.

As the hideous dragon
watched him, Jason aimed
his spear, ready to throw
it. Suddenly the dragon
sprang at him with
a roar!

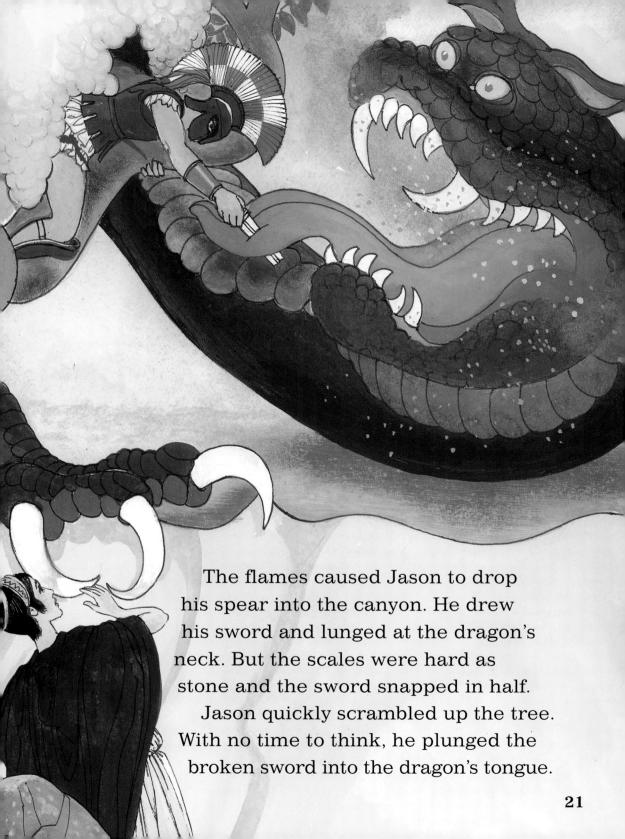

The flames caused Jason to drop
his spear into the canyon. He drew
his sword and lunged at the dragon's
neck. But the scales were hard as
stone and the sword snapped in half.
Jason quickly scrambled up the tree.
With no time to think, he plunged the
broken sword into the dragon's tongue.

Jason's broken sword stuck into the dragon's tongue and caused the dragon to pull away. The dragon roared with fury and flung its head side to side, trying to get rid of Jason's sword. Jason quickly grabbed the Golden Fleece and jumped out of the tree. He began to run, and the dragon chased after him.

"Quick," Jason shouted to Medea. "Come with me!"

Together, they raced down to the *Argo* and jumped on board.

"I have the prize!" Jason yelled to the Argonauts. "Let us return to Thebes!"

The Argonauts began to row with all their strength. Jason looked back. The dragon was on the beach, roaring at them in a fury.

When Jason and Princess Medea arrived in Thebes with the Golden Fleece, Pelias was amazed. He released Aeson from prison and handed him the crown.

As for Jason and Medea—they were soon married. Medea had her magic to help make them happy, but she never tired of admiring Jason's cloak, which he made out of the Golden Fleece.